Out of Shadows of Love

Tangra Delgado

OUT OF THE SHADOWS OF LOVE

<u>*These poems are for you*</u>

Feelings of love, loss, passion and pain, desire and emptiness…Salvation. Emotions felt by everyone, everywhere, all over the world. Written straight from the heart in plain words, for all to share.

Poems filled with the words we have all felt but could not say at some time, some place in our lives. Some of these poems will make you want to jump up and cry out because you now know that someone, somewhere has felt what you are feeling. You are NOT alone.

This book is written to everyone, everywhere, who has a heart. Written for all who have loved, lost and loved again.

LIFE ALWAYS GOES ON

Contents

Vow of Love

My Darling Love,

   This letter is written to let you know how happy I am to let you into my world. Looking to find you here, hoping I find you there, only to find that I haven't found you at all. You're just a dream. It looked like I was to spend the rest of my life alone, with no love meant just for me. Now here you stand before me. Looking into my eyes with a smile of true love upon your face. My promise to you, for as long as your love is true to me, is that I will love only you with each and every beat of my heart. For each and every day of my life I will work toward making all our dreams of love a reality. Welcome to my heart. Welcome to my world.

With All My Heart

True Love

True love
It's something hard to find
Everyone finds it easy to say
But meaning it is another thing

He shows his love to get your sex
You give your sex to get his love
Empty words to fill your mind
But true love is from the heart

It's when all you think about is him
Everything around reminds you of him
When harm comes his way
You go out of your mind until he is safe

True love
It will make you do things
Things you never dreamed you would do Like
dancing when there is no music

Just the thought of losing him
Makes a tear fall from your heart
That's when you know it's real
True love is in your heart

You just don't know about his love
It's a funny thing, true love
It's hard to get and harder to hold
It makes you wonder if there is true love

True love is in the heart of the one who loves.

Paradise

Come along with me
Let's take a trip
I want to show you another world
A place filled only with love

Where the birds sing songs of love
The sky is sunny and blue
We will be the only ones there
Just our little paradise

A place filled with roses and waterfalls
Perfect for a couple like you and I
It will be our little hideaway
A paradise made just for two

I'll give you all my heavenly treats
You may even drink the honeydew
From my special cup of love
That runs over just for you

Lick my honey to the last drop
For it will refill with just your touch
This is our private garden
I am your Eve and you're my Adam

There's no heartache or pain
No heartbreaks; no loneliness
Just you and I
Together as one

Making love in every way
From the darkest of night
Until the break of dawn
Here in our little paradise

Hear the Words I Say

Stop! Take a moment
To listen to the words I say
Hear my heart speaking to you
I'm not asking for the world
I only ask for all of your heart

I don't want any pretense
I don't need a show
Give me all the love you feel
Talk to me right from your heart
Be true to yourself and to me

If you can hear the words I say
My heart is telling you to be real
When you're true to yourself
You can be true to me too
Just listen to the words I say

True love begins within you
It's not what your friends say
It's not about past relationships
I'm not asking for the world
Only asking for all of your heart

The only way to give me your heart
Is to be true to you
The street can't teach what it doesn't know
Look within your heart
And let the real man grow

No need to pretend
No need to be hard
Everything you need
Is deep within your heart
Do you hear the words I say

Once you can be true to yourself
A new world will open up
A world like you've never known
There you will find true love
There you will find me

Unwanted Child

I've cried so many tears
Felt like I was a curse
How could anyone love me?
My own mother didn't want me
Gave me to another woman to raise
She told me day after day
That no one would have me
That I could only be a whore
She beat me every day
Left me marked from head to toe
No one reached out to help me
I dreamed of a better life
But it's hard to keep your head up
When someone keeps knocking it down
Using words of insult to keep me down
I believed those words for a long time
Always felt like the black sheep
Abused as a child
Abused as an adult
Always down but refusing to stay down
I had a dream of love
Having someone to love me

Someone to care for me
To teach me all about true love
I prayed for this and believed in it
Now the unwanted child cries no more
No tears of hurt from never knowing love
The unwanted child now knows true love
She's not unwanted anymore

My Husband

If I had my share of wishes
And wishes would come true
I'd wish that every woman
Could have a man like you

A knight in shining armor
The dream that did come true
The man that can light up her soul
Just by walking in the room

He can take her tear and fears away
Because she knows he's on her side
A gift sent down from heaven
Asking her to be his bride

That's the way you make me feel
Each time I see your face
I know that God has sent you
To put love in heartache's place

My heart knew only darkness and pain
Each day filled with sorrow and rain
Every day I thank God for you
My darling husband, my dream come true

Saddened

Tears falling from my eyes
Saddened for so many reasons
Sickness covers the earth
With this sickness comes death
This sickness is a plague
Some people, still trying to be players
Taking chances with their lives
I love my life and I want to live
Tears falling from my eyes
Saddened by the pain that covers
The earth more and more each day
No matter how safe you try to be
You've no idea what your partner does
When you're not around
I'm saddened by the deaths
Saddened for all the loved ones left behind
Tears falling from my eyes
Because the sickness is spreading
Even as we speak
As life goes on there's a chance
I could get this sickness
Just as easily as you

A punishment for our sins
Tears falling from my eyes
Saddened by the illness
That's causing so much death

Never Knew Love

Young woman
Who grew up in pain
Never knowing her mother's love
Grew up in a world of hurt
Always looking for a loving touch
So much love trapped within
Wishing upon the stars above
Praying love will find it's way in
Searching high and low
Only finding hurt and pain
Love only seems to come
Just to cut her down
Wondering why she was born
Was it just to be a stepping-stone
Seems everyone abuses her
Pain has become her best friend
When lovers leave
Pain is always there for her
Ave all she had inside
The world has turned her cold
Putting up her walls of protection

They can't see her hurt and pain
She closed herself off to the world
Where no one can cause her pain
Young woman who never knew love

Wake Up, My Brothers

Wake up my brothers
There's no time for sleeping
You've been sleeping far too long
I'm wondering what's going on
Where are the Martin Luther Kings?
What happened to the Malcolm X's?
Does anyone remember the dream?
There was a time when
The KKK used to kill our people
Now we just kill each other
When we're not killing each other
We're busy killing ourselves with drugs
Drug dealers walk around looking big
They're nothing but selfish murderers
Killing you off, slowly, day by day
What example are we giving
To the children of tomorrow?
Teach them to be lazy
Not to work and be a man
To be selfish just like you
Not to care for their fellow man
We have lots of fathers, but no daddies

How can you make a child
And the just walk away
Our people have given up
What happened to keeping hope alive?
We're like crabs is a basket
When one tries to climb out
The others pull it back down
When all we have to do
Is give each other a hand
So we'll all be free to move on
Instead we hold each other down
Of all the races on this earth
We're the hardest to get along
Wake up my brothers
You've been sleeping far too long
What happened to the Black Panthers?
Where are all the strong black men?
We wanted freedom for our people
And our people fought for years
Just for us to have that freedom
How have we repaid them?
By killing each other off
By killing ourselves and our future
Not caring for our children
Not caring for ourselves as a people

It's time to wake up
The million-man march was great
But one moment won't make a change
We need to come together
By any means necessary
Wake up my dear brothers
"Keep hope alive"
"Power to the people"
Wake up my brothers
You've been sleeping far too long
You've become slaves again
Slaves to hate, greed and selfishness
Wake up my brothers
The KKK stopped killing us
Have you ever wondered why?
It's because they don't have to
We do it to ourselves
We kill ourselves as a people
Better than anyone else
Wake up my brothers
The fight is not over
In fact, it's only just begun

Tonight

Tonight, there's only you and me
The world is at a stand still
As we start this journey to paradise
You take me, ever so gently, in your arms
Carry me to the land of love
The smell of roses fills the air
There's a glow of candlelight in the room
The feel of satin against my skin
As you lay me upon the sheets
As you caress my body, oh so tenderly
And your sweet lips so lovingly
Kiss each and every part of me
Chills run up and down my spine
I tremble all over, filled with desire
As our passions become one
Feeling as though we're on a cloud
Flowing to the heavens and stars above
When our loving comes to an end
We lay in each other's arms
Feeling like we are at heaven's door
It's as if it's just you and I
The world is at a stand still
Tonight we became as one

In Today's World

In today's world
It's hard to know right from wrong
You try to walk in the right path
But when you do, you end up hurt

You give all you have
Yet someone always wants more
You try to be nice and do right
Someone always gets in your way

You look to the heavens for answers
Yet answers don't fall from the sky
So much pain and sorrow in this world
You wonder when it will stop

It's not the world that's a mess
It's the people that are the problem
When will we change?
Look at who we are inside

Make changes as a people
For as a people we must change
Before we ever see a change
In today's world

Daddy

My Dearest Daddy,

Sitting here, thinking of how much I love you and how much you mean to me. I want to thank you for all you've done for me. No matter what happened, you were always there for me.

I've never told you this, but you mean the world to me. I look up to you because you've always been strong for me. You worked so hard to make sure I had the things I needed. You gave me everything I wanted.

When I'm asked what I look for in a man, my mind always goes back to you. I want a man that's as loving and caring as my daddy. I think God must have broken the mold when he made you because there is no one like my daddy. I love you, daddy, with all my heart.

Your Loving Daughter

What's Your Name?

In the morning sun
I see your face
With a warm glow
Surrounding you so gently

As we pass each other
I want to reach out to you
Just to say hello
What's your name?

Each time I try
My words get stuck inside
Only a silly smile
Makes it to my face

As you walk on by
Maybe one day
I'll have the nerve to say
What's your name?

Until that day comes
We will pass with a smile
While I still wonder
What's your name?

Raindrops & Teardrops

As the raindrops fall
So do the tears from my eyes
So many raindrops
So many tears

Just like the storm outside
There's a storm within my heart
But when the sun shines outside
The storm in my heart goes on

Every day is filled with teardrops
When will the sun shine for me?
When will my soul be filled with joy?
Will my heart ever know true love?

Will all my days be filled with pain?
The days are filled with storms
As the raindrops fall
So do the teardrops from my eyes

Never knew love could hurt so bad
Until the day you walked out on me

I didn't know my love for you ran so deep
Thought I could get over you

Since you went away
My life just hasn't been the same
From the world I hide my pain
But it feels like I'm going insane

Cry so hard
Feels like I'm going to die
Hurts so bad
Feels like I'll break in half

Never knew this kind of pain before
I used to have such control
Now it feels as though
I've reached the end of my rope

As the raindrops fall
So do the teardrops from my eyes
So much pain!
So much rain!

Ever since you walked out that door
My life just hasn't been the same

Listen to My Heart

Lay your head on my chest
Listen to my heart
I need you to under stand
Why the tears fall from my eyes

My heart is broken
You pushed my love away
I gave you all my time
Gave you all my love and understanding

You ripped my heart apart
After years of loving you
Planning my life around you
How do I make my love go away?

Lay your head on my chest
Listen to my heart
Tell me why you hurt me so
How could you put this pain inside me?

I gave you the best of my years
Listen to my heart
I want you to understand
All the words that I say

You gave me a taste of heaven
Now let me send you straight to hell!

Where Will It End?

Every day a gun is fired
Every day a child left dying
Every day a mother left crying
Where will it end?
It's all got to stop!
Every day a girl is crying
For she's just a child
And soon she'll be a mother
Where will it end?
It's all got to stop!
Every day there's a kid on the corner
Out to make a fast dollar
Selling drugs to his brothers and sisters
Where will it end?
It's all got to stop!
Every day hate grows stronger
Every day the world gets colder
Every day the end of time gets closer
Where will it end?
It's all got to stop!
Everyone's looking for something

Joy, happiness and love
STOP! Look at yourself
Look inside yourself and see
How special you are
Then you can see
How special others are
We're all God's children
We all have a purpose
We were put on this earth
To love one another
We have to change
Stop the hurt
Heal the pain
We have to start with ourselves
If we change from within
We will see things differently
In the world we live in
Where will it end?
It's all got to stop!

I Feel You, Still

In the stars
I can still see your face
Smiling back at me
In the wind
I can still hear your voice
Calling out my name
In the sunshine
I can feel the warmth
Of you standing next to me
In the rain
I can feel the tears
Falling from your face
We've both been hurt before
And the pain was too much to bear
But somehow we made through
Love is all we need
Even though life goes on
Without you at my side
I'll be looking for you
In the stars
I'll be listening for you
In the wind

I'll wait to feel your warmth
In the sunshine
I pray the rain never comes
That the pain stays away
Tonight, I'll be seeing you
In the stars

In the Back of My Mind

So many nights
I sit on my bed
Crying right through the night
I think of the day
When you'll come along
And whisper the words "I love you"

I guess it would help
If I knew who you were
But I don't even know your name
You have no face
You're just a wish
In the back of my mind

You don't have a name
And I don't know your face
And I haven't a clue where to start
I search for you
But you're just a wish
Deep in the back of my mind

So now it seems
That I must go on
Praying I'll run into you
Then you will be
More than a dream
Not a wish in the back of my mind

If There is Love

Life can be so hard
It can drive you out of your mind
Putting you through so many changes
Trying to find happiness
That doesn't seem to be
Anywhere to be found
Looking back at your life
Wondering where you went wrong
As the tears roll down your face
You find no answers
So you ask yourself
Where do I go from here?
Do I cut myself off from the world?
Do I dare try to love again?
Is there any such thing as love?
Is love just an ideal in our heads
Given to us in fairy tales?
I've looked to the stars
I've looked to the heavens
I've searched the whole world over
All I have found is hurt and pain
Lies and betrayal everywhere I looked

If there is true love
If there is happiness
It has never known me
My wish upon wish
Above all else
Is that love and happiness find me

Tears of Love

My Dearest Love,

Since you went away, I awaken to find tearstains on my pillow where I've cried myself to sleep. When you went away, I gave you a kiss. I was filled with pride and joy even though my heart was breaking to see you leave for war.

Each night I prayed that you would come home to me. Ever since you've been gone I have cried so many tears for, praying for your safe return. Even though I am filled with pride I am still filled with fear, bringing teardrops to my pillow.

Now that you're back, and your time in the war is over, my heart is filled with joy. My knight in shining armor is home and back in my arms. No more crying myself to sleep. Now my nights are filled with happiness, laughter, love and passion. My hero's back home, in my arms where you belong. I am so very happy and so much in love with you. Welcome back home to my arms.

Your Darling Love

From the wives and girlfriends of the soldiers at war.

Spell of Love

My love is sweet
Yet so deadly
Like the black widow spider

You can't hit and run
My poison works quickly
It draws you back, wanting me

My love is like voodoo
When I cast my
Spell of love on you

You lose all control
Hopelessly in love with me
Like and addict wanting more

My every wish
Becomes your command
It drives you out of your mind

You try to run
Only to find yourself running back
Under my spell of love

In Wonder

I couldn't fall asleep tonight
I have so much on my mind
Wondering how it feels
To love someone
Who loves you just as much
I wonder how true love feels
I wonder how it feels to awaken
And find the one you love
Laying next to you
Knowing his love for you is real
I wonder how it feels
To put your trust I someone
And never have to worry
I wonder how it would be
To find that special someone
That loves you no matter what
That special someone to love in return
With no fears between you
I'm dying to know
I have never had that love
I've never loved someone
That loved me just the same

I have shown love before
Never to be loved back
There were those who loved me
But I couldn't love them back
I want a relationship
Where we can love each other
I just wonder how it would feel
Now I sit here in wonder
Maybe one day I will know

Am I Wrong

Am I wrong?
Is true love
Different than I believe?
I believe two people
Should be in love with one another
Not one in love with the other
Both must love each other
Am I wrong?
Shouldn't love come from the heart?
Shouldn't it be able to bring out
All you have hidden inside?
Shouldn't it make you feel
Like you're on top of the world?
Am I wrong?
You should know true love
When it comes to you
You will be able to trust
And give yourself up totally
Am I wrong?
Is it that I don't know
What true love is at all?

I thought it was sharing and caring
Trusting and loving
Being open and honest with one another
Giving your all
But now I don't know
Tell me, am I wrong?

My Love is Real

I send a whisper in the wind
To tell you that I love you
I send you soft raindrops
To wash your tears away
I grow flowers for you
So you will smell love in the air
I give you the moon
So will know there's still light
Even in the darkest hours
I give you the morning sun
To brighten all your days
I give you the air you breathe
For it is like Me
Though you cannot see it
You know it's always there
I give you the trees
To shade you when it's hot
I give you the stars
Just to make you smile
I give you all these things
Made especially for you

So you will know I love you
And My love is real
These are a taste of Heaven on Earth
Until the day when I return

Close Your Eyes

Come my darling
Close your little eyes
As I sing you a lullaby
Enter the world of fairytales

Dream of candy canes and lollipops
Teddy bears and water slides
Dream of a world of joy and laughter
Enter the land of fairytales

Close your little eyes
And know you are safe
The apple of mama's eyes
You have my heart in your hand

Don't you cry, don't be afraid
Know my love belongs to you
So close your eyes my little one
Dream a dream of happiness

Close your eyes
And enjoy your dreams
Don't you worry or be afraid
Mama's love will be here for you

Momma, Come Home

I woke up this morning
To find you had gone
Looked everywhere to see your face
Thought you might have gone to the store
But days passed and you never came back

I don't know what I did wrong
Whatever it was, I'm so sorry
I promise to be good for you
I miss you and need you
Momma, please come home

I try hard to do everything right
I don't cry, I hold my tears in
Don't make noise when I'm playing
I do as I'm told; all I want is your love
So please momma, please come home

They told me you didn't want me
I just can't understand why
It can't be true, momma
I love you so much
Please momma, come home to me

Right Out of Heaven

Dearest Husband,

The day you put this ring on my finger, you promised to love me always. You promised to cherish me forever, letting no other come between us. Standing before God and everyone around us, you sealed your love for me with a kiss. I never dreamed it would be this way. You took all my dreams of love to a whole new level. I never dreamed I could be loved this way. The years have passed us by and you have surpassed all of my dreams. I thank God so many times for you. The love you've not only given, but also shown me makes me feel like you stepped right out of heaven. You stepped right up to my front door, just for me. Each day you act as if it were the first day we met. You polish me up each day with your love. You make each day feel like our wedding day and each night feel like our honeymoon. You're the husband that walked right out of heaven, into the arms of a woman that loves you with all her heart. Thank God for sending you to me.

Your Loving Wife

Dreamer

As a child
I always looked to the stars
Dreaming of how life would be
I looked at how pretty the stars were
At how wonderful the world was
As a child
Everything was new and fresh
Each day was an adventure
There was nothing you couldn't try
If it didn't work, just try something new
As a child
Some days I felt I could reach out
All the way to the sky
I often wondered how the stars
Made it up so high
As a child
I dreamed that one day
I'd live on the Milky Way
I was such a dreamer
I had so many dreams
Never feared trying to
Make them come true

As a woman
I want to dream again
Not be afraid to chase my dreams
Without fear of failing
I want to get up and try again
To dream as a child was wonderful
But I'm not a child anymore
I do have many dreams
As a woman
I'm going after my dreams now

Parents of Yesterday

I see children today
Running wild in the streets
Eight-year-old girls
Wearing thongs for all to see
Little three-year-old boys
Ask if you want to buy weed
Where are the parents of yesterday?
They had time to teach their kids
When everyone knew who the parent was
And it certainly wasn't the child
These days, parents don't know
Where the kids are, most of the time
And the kids don't know
Where their parents are
Or does anyone even care?
Then when the child
Ends up dead or in jail
The parents are quick to cry
How did you end up this way?
Ask yourself this
Where were you when your child grew up?
Did you teach them right from wrong?

Or did the streets teach them
While you were out partying
With all your friends?
Parents of yesterday
Knew every step their child took
Because they were right there with them
Talk grown if dared
You got a smack in the mouth
Kids didn't end up in jail like now
Because the parents then
Were real, full time, parents
Not only when the mood hit them
Our children are suffering
Where are the parents of yesterday?

Thank You

You walked into my life
Giving all of yourself to me
Problems came your way
Yet you faced all at my side
When I felt weak
You held me up
And made me feel strong again
When tears rolled from my eyes
You were there to wipe them away
You knew the words to give me hope
I'd looked for love so long
I prayed to the Lord above
And he sent you just for me
When ever you walk into the room
Every part of me leaps for joy
My eyes light up
When I see your face
You're always so gentle and sweet
And you don't just say you love me
You show it in all that you do
Each night, when I pray
I thank the Lord for your love

We've been together for a while now
But with you every day's like the first
The first time we became one
I thank God for your love
And I thank you for loving me

Baby Girl

Baby girl, your eyes are so bright
Smile so big it could melt the world
So happy at every little thing
That she learns to do
Has so much faith in mom and dad
Watching every move that you make
Learning everything that you do
Watch out, baby girl is copying you
All she knows is what she sees you do
She hears the music and it gets in her feet
Always doing something to see you smile
For every step you take
Baby girl takes two
Oh my little baby girl
Why do you grow so fast?
Holding you in my arms
You playing kissy-face or peek-a-boo
I still remember
When you took your first step
Baby girl, baby girl
How did you grow so fast?
Just yesterday you lost your first tooth

And now you're becoming a bride
Where did the time go?
It went by so fast
Baby girl, baby girl
You're all grown up
But no matter what
You're still my baby girl

Look At My Son

Look at my son
Yesterday you were playing with sticks
Running around chasing frogs
Racing up and down on your bike
Tormenting your sisters left and right
Playing jokes on everyone you saw
My how you've grown
So big and strong
Once my little baby
Crawling on the floor
Running naked down the hall
Driving me crazy
With cuts and falls
Making up games with your friends
Getting in all kinds of mess
Once a silly baby
Then a goofy teen
Making your sisters crazy
Trying to be the big brother
How you've grown
So big and tall
Serving your country

Protecting us all
Grown from a boy to a man
Standing strong in your uniform
Sailing the waters from coast to coast
As I look back
On all the years passed
A tear comes to my eyes
And filled with pride
I look at my son
How big and strong
You are a man
Who can hold your own
You fill my heart
With joy and laughter
You fill my soul
With love and pride
Look at my son
Standing tall and strong

In Hell

Having your life threatened
Having a man choke you
He puts a gun to your head
And in your stomach so hard
That it leaves a mark
He talks down to you
Making your life a living hell
He says you deserve it
He says that you hurt him
Because you made him love you
Now he has to serve you justice
His kind of justice
Because you didn't smile or talk
When you did talk
You didn't say what he wanted to hear
You don't live your life
The way he feels you should live it
So you're not living right in his eyes
He's appointed himself your God
When he says so you will die
If you tell anyone
About the way he treats you

He will kill you
You're his to do with
Whatever he wants
You must take whatever he dishes out
It means nothing for him to abuse you
In his eyes that's what you're for
When he wants to, he beats you
And when he's done you're to get over it
Forget all about it
And give your love to him
If you ever loved someone
That love never leaves you
No matter what they do
These are the things he tells you
You can't stop loving someone
No matter what they do to you
That's not true love
But that's what he wants you to believe
He calls you all of the thing that he is
Evil, selfish, a dog and worthless
He says that if you listen to him
Maybe you'll get somewhere in life
Before him your bills got paid
Before him your kids had clothes
You got some of the things you wanted

Now you have bill on top of bills
You're very unhappy; you have no life
All you have left is a prayer
Never to see his face again
You try to find ways to pay the bills
So you don't have to ask him for anything
The phone gets cut off and
The cable will follow soon behind
You try to keep it on
But you'll sacrifice your body
Before you ask for his help
You borrow money to help him out
To get yourself out of the mess
Now you're a queen in his eyes
When the money is gone
You're lower than dirt
And the bills pile up again
Before he was around
You had no real problems
Now you're in way over your head
Always suffering heartache
Pain and threats are your companions
You have no life of your own
The police can do but so much
And it's not nearly enough

Sure they will put him in jail
But his family will just get him out
Then your family will be all dressed up
In their best black suits and dresses
Find someone else?
Why would he?
He has the perfect puppet here
Right where he wants you to be
In hell with no way out
You have your children
You want to bring them up
You have no money
You have no place to go
No one to help you out of this hell
What do you do?
How can you get out?
How can you leave and still stay alive?
How can you get out of harm's way?
How do you get him out of your life?
Do you try to kill him?
No, you can't go to jail
For your children's sake
In jail your life wouldn't be any different
You would still want to be free
If you try to run

He will find you
Whatever it takes
Do you dare to ask for help?
If you dare then whom do you ask?
Who can you turn to
That will save you from him
You can take the chance
For there are those who will listen
There are those who truly love you
And when there seems to be no hope
You can turn to God
He is always there when you need Him
I took the chance
Now I thank God
For I am free from hell

The Perfect Husband

I had given up on love
But only in my mind
In my heart it was my desire
I prayed to the Lord
With all of my heart
Asked the Lord for just what I wanted
It was hard to believe
When you walked into my life
You came giving me the love
I had only dreamed of
A man that loves me for me
That loves me just as I am
No trying to change me
Accepts my faults with the good
He's always there for me, at my side
I couldn't ask for a better husband
My wants, my needs, my desires
I find them all
Every time I look in your eyes
I searched all my life
And now I have found you
The perfect husband

Father's House

Hush, don't cry for me
Now is the time to rejoice
I lived a long, happy life
I lived my life as I chose
I was your mother
I was your grandmother
Your sister, your aunt
Your friend and neighbor
Your loving wife
I loved the man of my dreams
Who loved me 'til death did we part
He stood at my side
To the very end
Don't cry for me
I've gone to my Father's house
My time hasn't ended
It has only just begun
In my heavenly Father's house
A place that knows no hurt or pain
I love you all so very much
So be happy that I've made it home
No more tears now

Just rejoice for me
I am happy now
At home in my father's house
Waiting for the day
When I greet you again
When I welcome you to my father's house

Missing You

Sometimes it feels like
You are still here with me
When I sleep at night
I dream I'm in your arms
I found one of your shirts
Just the other day
I could smell your cologne
And the tears rolled from my face
The pain was fresh once more
Like I had lost you all over again
It's been a half a year now
But it feels like yesterday
I look to the heavens
With a smile on my face
I know I'll see you again
I know you watch over me
You are the love of my life
And the most wonderful man I know
I will live my life
As lovingly as you did
So we will meet again in heaven

Save a seat next to you for me
I will love you 'til we meet again
I miss you my love

Grateful

You stepped into my life
Showing nothing but understanding
Sharing happiness and tenderness
The things I've always wanted
But I have never known
All I ever got from men was
Hurt, disappointment and heartache
I cried out to God above
To send me someone I could love
That would love me in return
Just for being me
Someone that loves God and me alone
The last place I would think of was
The very place you were waiting
You've given me the love
I thought I could only dream of
Now I want everyone to know
The love you've given me
I thank God for giving me the chance
To know a love as pure as yours
May this love last until the end of time
I thank God for your love
And I thank you for loving me

Pure Love

Time keeps on changing
Nothing stays the same
With each day that passes
Changes are made
We grow a little older
A new life is born
Another life is lost
Someone falls in love
Someone else's heart is broken
A soul has been saved
Another has been lost
Time keeps on changing
Things come and go
No matter how things change
Love lives on forever
Because God is pure love
And pure love will never die
So if your love for me is pure
And my love for you is pure
Our love will last for eternity
I thank God for a love so pure
Pure love is what I found in you

Little Star

My Little Star
Your eyes shine so bright
When I look at you
I see a model
Maybe even a movie star
With your name in lights
I'll teach you to be strong
To hold your head up high
Not to depend on others
To be a woman
That stands all on her own
Not to be with someone
Because she has to be
But because she wants to be
I'll prepare you for the real world
Because the world owes you nothing
But be determined to make it
Letting nothing stand in your way
My Little Star
Will always shine bright
And will always be
My little starlight
Shining so bright

Printed in the United Kingdom
by Lightning Source UK Ltd.
103153UKS00003B/289